The gir'
who could be anything

Author: Peter A Johnson

Illustrator: Tamara Piper

I could be a pirate,
The ruler of the seas,
Sailing through the water,
Fighting enemies.

Find the buried treasure,
Hidden beneath the sand,
Sail the seven seas,
Discovering new lands.

I could be a knight,
Wearing armour nice and proud,
Charging on my horse,
With the crowd cheering loud.

Protect my king and country,
Defend the castle every day,
Save the sick and help the poor,
In every little way.

I could be a fire fighter,
Stop the houses burning down,
Turn on and ring the siren,
Save all the lives in town.

See a burning building,
I wouldn't be so scared,
Put out the flames and
stop the smoke,
Show everyone I cared.

I could be a mountaineer,
Conquer higher ground,
Reach the top of every tip,
And see for miles around.

Nothing could ever stop me,
The places I could go,
Climbing up, all around,
Walking through the snow.

I could be a builder,
Creating what I like,
Stacking up the bricks,
Until they reach the sky.

Building strong homes,
For families to live,
Being proud of what I've made,
And all the love I give.

I could be a famous footballer,
Running down the wing,
Every time I scored a goal,
The crowd would cheer and sing.

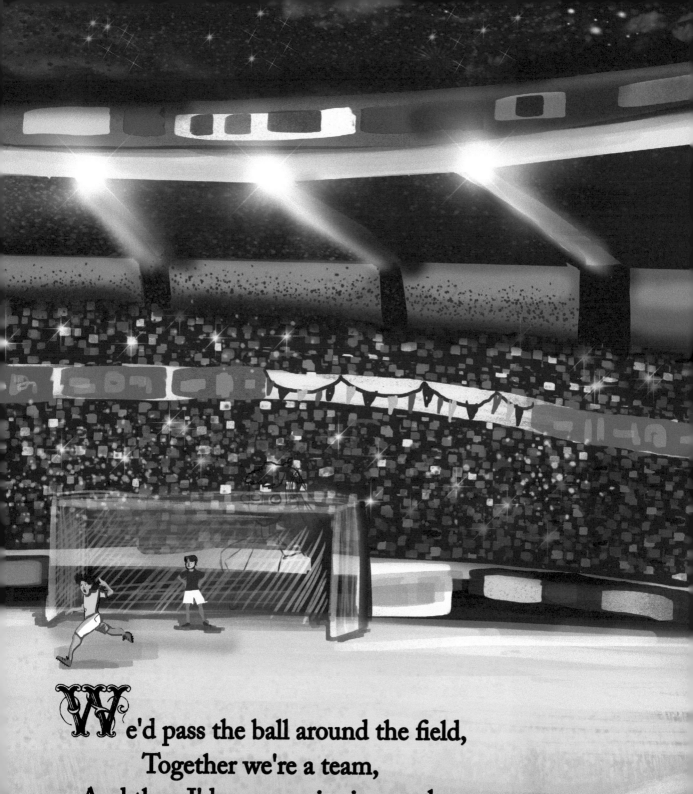

We'd pass the ball around the field,
Together we're a team,
And then I'd score a winning goal,
That would be my dream.

I could be an astronaut,
Shoot right up into space,
Discover brand new planets,
Would really be quite ace.

Sitting in my rocket.
Space rocks flying by,
Looking down on Earth,
Seeing beauty in the skies.

I could be a scientist,
Curing a disease,
Mixing lots of potions,
With my expertise.

earing my white coat,
Goggles and a smile,
I would make something so special,
Every once in a while.

I could be a racing driver,
At the starting line,
I'd feel the rev of the engine,
As it tingled up my spine.

The lights turn green and off we go,
We're speeding down the track,
I'm sure to be the winner,
As I complete another lap.

I could be a pilot,
Gliding in a plane,
Soaring over fields,
Over France and Spain.

I could travel to wherever,
I would surely make the time,
Every destination,
Would really be sublime.

I could look after animals,
I could be a vet,
Treating injured doggies,
And all the other pets.

I'd learn their names and stroke their fur,
Give them what they'd need,
I'd also pat them on theirs heads,
When they get to leave.

I could be a teacher,
Teaching right from wrong,
To work out all the answers,
We could sing a little song.

I'd teach them how to count,
Write and exercise,
Become an artist with their brush,
Set them up for life.

You know what
now I think of it,
I could be anything,
If I put my mind to it,
I could even learn to sing.

I really must remember,
To build my self-esteem,
And anything is possible,
When little children dream.

If you enjoyed the book, please be kind enough to leave a review on Amazon.

Reviews are really important as they help other readers find out more about the book. The more readers there are, the more people the story will reach.

You can follow the author on social media using the handle @pajthewriter on all of the platforms below.

Why not give other wonderful stories written by Peter A Johnson a try!